LOVE WELL
~ MY ~
PRECIOUS ONE

Words by
Jill Roman Lord

Illustrations by
Camila Carrossine

End Game Press books may be purchased in bulk at special discounts for sales promotion, corporate gifts, ministry, fund-raising, or educational purposes. Special editions can also be created to specifications. For details, contact Special Sales Dept., End Game Press, P.O. Box 206, Nesbit, MS 38651 or info@endgamepress.com.

Visit our website at www.endgamepress.com.

Library of Congress Control Number: 2022952422
Hardback ISBN: 978-1-63797-083-6
eBook ISBN: 978-1-63797-084-3

Published in association with Cyle Young of the Cyle Young Literary Elite, LLC.

Illustrations by: Camila Carrossine, Bright Agency
Design by Monica Thomas for TLC Book Design, TLCBookDesign.com

Printed in China
10 9 8 7 6 5 4 3 2 1

TO THE LOVE OF MY LIFE, BILL.
THANK YOU FOR YOUR CONSTANT
LOVE & SUPPORT.

God blessed you
with a great big heart.
He made you sensitive and smart.

I wonder how
you'll do your part?
Love well, my precious one.

When you receive a teddy bear
    or doll to love and comb her hair,
it's yours to treat with tender care.
Love well, my precious one.

Someday you'll learn to share your toys.
That's how to play with girls and boys.
You'll soon discover many joys!
Love well, my precious one.

You'll play with friends, and if they pout,
or disagree, and stomp or shout,
I hope you'll calmly talk it out.
Love well, my precious one.

Include new children in your game.
 If you don't know them, ask their name.
You'd like for them to do the same.
 Love well, my precious one.

If friends hit home runs past the wall,
but you can't seem to hit the ball,
still say, "Good job!" Keep standing tall.
Love well, my precious one.

But if you score the winning goal,
    don't boast and brag or lose control.
You play together as a whole.
    Love well, my precious one.

Be sure to make your bed each day,
and clean your room, put toys away.
It shows your love when you obey.
Love well, my precious one.

If Grandpa's sick and needs to rest,
then draw a card and do your best.
That's sure to make him feel so blessed.
Love well, my precious one.

Perhaps a baby comes along,
    takes Mommy's time, which seems so wrong.
        Still know you're loved and must be strong.
        Love well, my precious one.

And if a puppy comes your way,
    then you can teach him how to play,
to fetch, and heel, and learn to stay.
    Love well, my precious one.

Enjoy God's world and show you care
by cleaning trash up here and there.
Plant flower seeds to add a flare!
Love well, my precious one.

Sometimes Mom makes you clean out stuff
and giving it away feels rough,
it blesses kids without enough.
Love well, my precious one.

You see, love tends to spread and grow,
prompts other people's love to show.
How far it goes, you'll never know.

Love well, my precious one.

A new command I give you: Love one another.
As I have loved you, so you must love one another.
–JOHN 13:34 (NIV)

Jill Roman Lord is a wife, mother of three amazing kids, runner, author, writer, nurse anesthetist, and Jesus lover. Jill is the author of several award-winning books. It is her desire in her writing to draw children closer to Jesus and to provide books that parents (or grandparents or caregivers) can enjoy reading with the kids snuggled on their laps. Find out more about her at jillromanlord.com.